MW00800833

Song of the
Last Miguel

Carol P. Saul illustrated by Minh Uong

Whispering Coyote Press, Inc. Boston

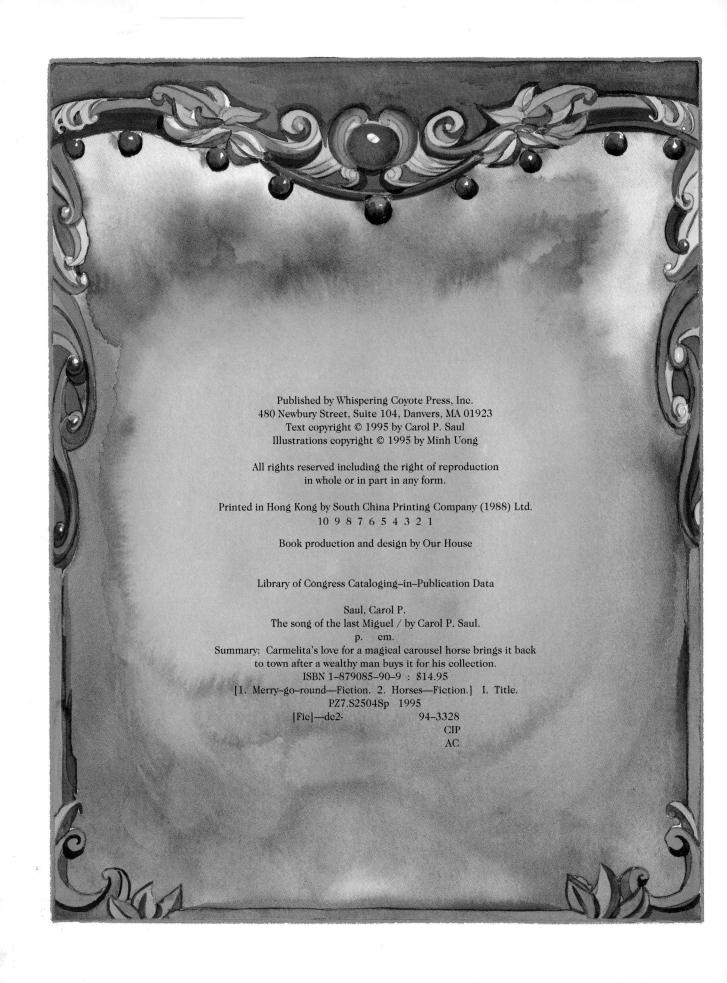

Published by Whispering Coyote Press, Inc.
480 Newbury Street, Suite 104, Danvers, MA 01923
Text copyright © 1995 by Carol P. Saul
Illustrations copyright © 1995 by Minh Uong

Printed in Hong Kong by South China Printing Company (1988) Ltd.
10 9 8 7 6 5 4 3 2 1

Book production and design by Our House

Library of Congress Cataloging–in–Publication Data

Saul, Carol P.
The song of the last Miguel / by Carol P. Saul.
p.   cm.
Summary: Carmelita's love for a magical carousel horse brings it back
to town after a wealthy man buys it for his collection.
ISBN 1–879085–90–9 : $14.95
[1. Merry–go–round—Fiction. 2. Horses—Fiction.] I. Title.
PZ7.S2504Sp 1995
[Fic]—dc2·   94–3328
                                         CIP
                                         AC

For Sid
—C.P.S.

To Suzanne
for her support and encouragement
—M.U.

In the plaza of Carmelita's town stood a red and gold carousel with twelve fine wooden horses. The finest of them all, the one the children loved best, was Miguel.

Miguel was the only horse whose name was carved into his mane,

but that is not why the children loved him. The children loved Miguel
because he could sing—not from his mouth, but from his heart.
Miguel's song was a faint, sweet sound that made every child who heard
it feel safe, happy, and loved.

Carmelita was little, and did not often get to hear Miguel's song. Other children always ran to him first. But sometimes old Señor Perez, who ran the carousel, would lift her up and put her on Miguel's back. How happy she was as she hugged his cream-colored mane and listened to his song! There was no sound Carmelita loved more, except for her own mother's voice.

One day Carmelita's mother took her to the train station. People were waving handkerchiefs and singing songs of farewell.

"Wave good-bye, little bird," said Carmelita's mother. "Señor Perez is going south to live with his daughter. He says he is too old to run the carousel anymore. Look, his train is leaving. *Adiós*, Señor Perez!"

Carmelita waved as Señor Perez's train disappeared. She tugged at her mother's shawl. "Mama," she asked, "who will run the carousel now?"

"Someone will surely come along," replied her mother.

But no one did.

At first the children still came, jumping up on the horses and urging them to go. But no one turned the crank of the motor, and the horses did not move. Soon the children climbed down and went away.

The red and gold paint faded. The horses' silver poles began to rust. Everyone forgot about the carousel—everyone except Carmelita.

She had grown tall, and her legs now dangled past the stirrups of Miguel's saddle. Still she came to sit on Miguel's back and lean against his mane, dreaming of his song.

"*Ay,* Carmelita and her horse!" her friends teased. "Come on! Forget about that old thing!"

"I will never forget," Carmelita said.

One day a man in a white suit got off the train. "Have you a carousel in this town?" he asked.

Carmelita followed the crowd that led the man to the plaza. The man climbed onto the carousel and inspected each horse. When he got to Miguel, he said, "Aha!"

"Señor," asked Carmelita, "do you fix carousels?"

"No, my dear," he replied. "I collect carousel horses. I own every horse made with the name 'Miguel' carved into its mane, except for this last one. Now that I have found it, I wish to buy it."

The man reached into his pocket and brought out such a large
wad of money that the crowd gasped.

"Will you sell this Miguel to me?" he asked.

"No!" cried Carmelita, but the buzz of the crowd drowned
her out.

"So much money!"

"We could fix up the town with that money!"

"Send for the mayor! Send for the mayor!"

"Wait!" said Carmelita. "What will happen to Miguel?"

"He will be cleaned and painted," the man replied. "Then he will be put in a large room with the rest of my collection. Every day I look at my Miguels. Perhaps one day you will come and look at them, too."

"But will no one ride on his back?" asked Carmelita. "Will no one lean against his mane and hear his song?"

"Song?" said the man. "What song, my dear?"

The mayor made his way through the crowd. He held up his hands for silence. "Let us vote," he shouted. "Who wants to sell?"

A forest of hands went up.

"Who does not want to sell?"

Carmelita raised her hand.

The mayor looked at Carmelita. Then he bowed to the man in the white suit. "Señor, the horse is yours."

The next day a red truck roared into the plaza. Carmelita watched three workers unbolt Miguel from his spot, load him into the truck, and drive away.

"*Adiós*, Miguel," she whispered.

Carmelita walked through the plaza with her head down. All around her people were arguing.

"Let us buy benches for the plaza," someone suggested.

"No, we must fix up the school," someone else said.

"No, no! We should put up a statue of the mayor!"

That evening Carmelita said to her mother, "Mama, the town should use the money to fix up the carousel."

"*Ay*, Carmelita," said her mother. "No one can run that old carousel anymore and no one wants to ride it."

"I do," said Carmelita.

"Ah, my dove," sighed her mother. "When I was a child, I, too, loved riding Miguel. But I grew up and left him behind me. Now, so must you."

"Why, Mama?" sobbed Carmelita. "Why must I?"

Weeks passed. One day the mayor called the townspeople to the plaza.

"We have decided how to spend the money from the sale of the horse Miguel," he began.

But before he could finish, the red truck roared into the plaza and the man in the white suit got out. Three workers lifted something out

of the truck. Carmelita could hardly believe her eyes. It was Miguel, as shiny as new!

The mayor hurried toward the man in the white suit.

"Good day, Señor," he said. "What can I do for you?"

"I am returning your Miguel," said the man. "He does not want to be in my collection."

"Ah—how do you know this, Señor?" asked the mayor.

"Because," said the man, "I heard him cry."

"What!" gasped the crowd.

"It is true," he continued. "I had him cleaned and painted and placed in my collection. How fine he looked! But every time I went to see my Miguels, I kept hearing a faint, sad sound. Where did it come from? Finally I leaned my head against his mane and heard it. This Miguel was crying!"

"No!" said the mayor.

"Yes," said the man in the white suit. "I called in experts. No one had ever heard of such a thing."

"But of course, Señor," Carmelita cried, "if a horse can sing, he can cry, too."

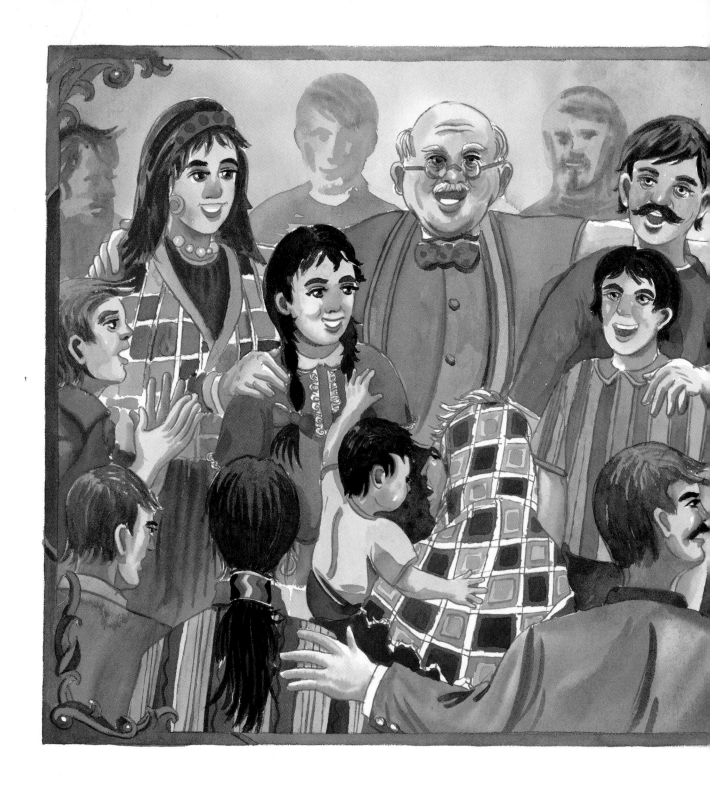

"Sing?" said the man. "A wooden horse cannot sing."

"Our Miguel sings," said Carmelita. "A faint, sweet sound. It always made me feel happy and loved. Listen, Señor." And she began to hum.

"I remember now," said a voice from the crowd.

"How I loved that sound, when I was a child!"

"And I," said someone else. "It made me feel safe and happy." He began to hum along. Another voice joined in. Soon the whole crowd was singing and swaying.

"One moment!" said the mayor. The humming stopped.

"If Miguel has returned to us," he said, "we must return the money. Is that not right, Señor?"

The crowd held its breath. The man in the white suit looked at the crowd, and then at Carmelita. "Keep the money," he said. "Fix the carousel."

The crowd cheered. The mayor held up his hands.

"But, Señor," said the mayor. "Since Señor Perez left, there is no one in our town to run the carousel."

"There is now," said a creaky voice. At the edge of the crowd, leaning on the arm of a much younger man, was old Señor Perez.

"Señor Perez!" Carmelita cried. She ran to hug him.

"I could not stay away," he said. "I missed the children. I missed the horses. I taught my grandson all I know about carousels. He will help me run it. But it needs work."

"I will help you!" cried Carmelita.

"And I!" said the man in white.

"And I! And I!" shouted others. Soon the plaza was filled with people

hammering and painting. By the end of the day, the carousel was ready.
Young Señor Perez took hold of the crank. He
pushed and strained. Very slowly, the carousel began to turn.

The crowd cheered. The children raced for the horses. Carmelita leaped onto Miguel's back and leaned against his cream-colored mane. Once more that faint, sweet sound was heard—the song of the last Miguel.